HURRICANE MUSIC

by **Barbara Bottner**

illustrated by **Paul Yalowitz**

G. P. Putnam's Sons   New York

Text copyright © 1995 by Barbara Bottner

Illustrations copyright © 1995 by Paul Yalowitz

All rights reserved. This book, or parts thereof, may not be reproduced
in any form without permission in writing from the publisher.
G. P. Putnam's Sons, a division of The Putnam & Grosset Group,
200 Madison Avenue, New York, NY 10016.
Published simultaneously in Canada.
Printed in Hong Kong by South China Printing Co. (1988) Ltd.
Type design by Patrick Collins
The text is set in Berkeley Oldstyle Medium.
Library of Congress Cataloging-in-Publication Data
Bottner, Barbara. Hurricane music / by Barbara Bottner;
illustrated by Paul Yalowitz.   p.   cm.
Summary: Aunt Margaret's discovery of an old clarinet
in the basement sets off a musical lifestyle for her and her
family that includes jamming with hurricanes.
[1. Music—Fiction. 2. Clarinet—Fiction.
3. Hurricanes—Fiction. 4. Aunts—Fiction.]
I. Yalowitz, Paul, ill. II. Title.   PZ7.B6586Hu   1995
[E]—dc20   92-43697 CIP AC
ISBN 0-399-22544-7
1   3   5   7   9   10   8   6   4   2
First Impression

For those who sing to me and with me:
Gerald Kruglik, Irving & Roz Bottner, Arthur Levine,
Joanne Kay, Ricki, Gloria, Jeff, Gert & Mike,
Kelly, Sandra Kagan, Carol, Diana, Irv & Shari.

—B.B.

To my nephew, Steven.

—P.Y.

One spring day my aunt Margaret found an old clarinet in the basement. She dusted it off, twisted the mouthpiece on and attached the reed. She covered the holes with her fingers, took a deep breath and blew.

"Merciful melodies!" she cried. "This is for me!"

Mostly she practiced her scales in the hall closet, so she wouldn't bother my uncle Seymour.

But one day Aunt Margaret realized she couldn't learn about music from inside a closet. "Seymour," she said, "since we can't afford music lessons, I'm going to study the sounds of life."

Aunt Margaret took me and her clarinet to the animal hospital where she used to work. She listened to the meows and the growls of the cats and dogs. "Raaaphhhh," went her old clarinet.

Two Dalmatians tried to sing along.

"Holy Faloozala! This is a blast," said Aunt Margaret.

On Saturday, we went to the railroad station. The conductor went "Toooot," and Aunt Margaret answered "Toootattoooo."

The train went "clack a-chooo, clack a-choo."

Aunt Margaret played faster.

The train picked up speed.

"I'm beginning to understand tempo," Aunt Margaret told Uncle Seymour that evening.

"Congratulations," sighed Uncle Seymour.

He didn't look happy to me.

On Sunday we packed a picnic lunch and hiked down an old mountain trail. But no sooner did Uncle Seymour spread out the chicken and raisin salad than Aunt Margaret was down by the stream.

First she listened, then she played.

The glistening water sprayed over the rocks as if lifted up by her notes.

"Gotta dance, gotta sing, gotta do my thing-a-ling," sang Aunt Margaret.

Uncle Seymour shook his head.

Monday was a holiday. Uncle Seymour asked Aunt Margaret to
take the day off. So we all put on our strawhats and drove to the
center of town.

It was morning, and the streets were quiet.

But at noon the church bells rang.

Giggling children rushed out to see the parade. A truck honked at a red light, and a man selling hot dogs shouted, "Get 'em right here...."

Before Uncle Seymour and I could stop her, Aunt Margaret picked up her clarinet and dazzled us with a tune.

"Whistling Winnebago!" she hollered. Passersby began to leap
and dance. Aunt Margaret's notes climbed higher and higher.
A policeman blew his whistle. Aunt Margaret wove all the sounds together
in a helter-skelter city song. Trees swayed, leaves jiggled on their branches.
   "Something has got to give!" moaned Uncle Seymour.

What gave was the weather.
Hurricane Gladys flew inland that night.
Everyone shut the windows, put on their fluffy
slippers and sipped steaming hot tea.
Everyone except my aunt. "Thundering horses couldn't
keep me from jamming with a hurricane!" She rushed outdoors
into the pelting rain.

"I married a wild woman,"
said my worried uncle.
Aunt Margaret was having a blast.
The more she played, the more the wind whipped through
the village, clattering the shutters and rattling the street signs.
Thunder erupted. The tempest shattered into a blinding downpour.
"I wish she'd come inside," said Uncle Seymour.

Just then a soaking wet Aunt Margaret stumbled into the house.

"Are you all right?" we asked.

"Dearest Seymour, this is the *endsville!* My horn *blew away!*"

And Aunt Margaret wept.

By Friday, Uncle Seymour was weeping too.

"Musicians must make music," he explained to me. "Now it's *too* quiet at our house."

To cheer everyone up, I invited Uncle Seymour and Aunt Margaret to our favorite ice-cream parlor. But out in the street we could hear the wailing of a fire truck's siren and jump ropes beating out a double-dutch rhythm. This time Aunt Margaret didn't say "Eat my hat, Pat!" She wouldn't touch her Chocolate Delight.

That evening Uncle Seymour and I painted signs.

By dinnertime the townspeople had turned up two old cat collars with bells, three sets of chattering false teeth, a ticking clock, several broken records, a windup doll that cried "Mama" and a music box. Everyone found something, but nobody found the clarinet.

All the next day, poor Aunt Margaret stared out the window.
No one had even heard so much as a "peachy keen" from her lips
since Hurricane Gladys had come and gone.

Something had to happen, but what? I told my aunt and uncle
to meet me at Finnegan's Music Store.

"Here is twenty-five cents. I would like a red harmonica,
please," I told Mr. Finnegan.

He handed it to me. It was new and pretty. I knew where
it belonged.

"Testifying troubadours!" Aunt Margaret pursed her lips together. She put everything she had into the tiny instrument. The first few notes were high and squeaky. Outside, the wind began to blow. At first it was just the gentlest of breezes.

Aunt Margaret was only getting started: Her song trilled and vibrated; it echoed and sizzled. The wind began to bang and howl and roar. The air turned cold and raindrops bounced as high as a dog's nose.

FREE
LESSONS
WITH
ANY
PURCHASE

SPECIAL

"We'd better bolt the windows tight," Uncle Seymour warned
Mr. Finnegan. "When Margaret plays, everything lets loose!"
Gladys's twin brother, Hurricane Harold, swept into town,

and he was ferocious!

Even with the small harmonica, Aunt Margaret was jazzed.
She wove her frenzied notes into the raging downpour.

The walls shook and warbled. It was terrific! Everyone waited to see what the hurricane would do next.

Then the front door crashed open. Something tumbled onto the floor of Mr. Finnegan's store. Muddy and tarnished, but with all its keys and pads intact, lay Aunt Margaret's clarinet.

Water dribbled out everywhere, but Aunt Margaret tenderly picked up her instrument and dried it off.

"Sanctifying Satchmo!" she hollered, and she invented a tune right there in the middle of Hurricane Harold. But this time the melody was tranquil and soothing.

The thunder became a distant rumble and the tumultuous storm began to subside. By midnight, Harold had become nothing more than a mild and steady drizzle.

Uncle Seymour took us all home and made peppermint tea.

Before I went to sleep, Aunt Margaret folded my hands around the red harmonica.

"What do you say?" asked Uncle Seymour.

I said, "Dancing Dinglediddy!" Of course.